SANCTUARY SOMEWHERE

BRENNA DIMMIG

An imprint of Enslow Publishing

WEST **44** BOOKS™

Please visit our website, www.west44books.com.
For a free color catalog of all our high-quality books,
call toll free 1-800-542-2595 or fax 1-877-542-2596.

Cataloging-in-Publication Data

Names: Dimmig, Brenna.
Title: Sanctuary somewhere / Brenna Dimmig.
Description: New York : West 44, 2019. | Series: West 44 YA verse
Identifiers: ISBN 9781538382837 (pbk.) | ISBN 9781538382844
  (library bound) | ISBN 9781538383421 (ebook)
Subjects: LCSH: Children's poetry, American. | Children's poetry,
  English. | English poetry.
Classification: LCC PS586.3 S263 2019 | DDC 811'.60809282--dc23

First Edition

Published in 2019 by
Enslow Publishing LLC
101 West 23rd Street, Suite #240
New York, NY 10011

Editor: Caitie McAneney
Designer: Seth Hughes

Printed in the United States of America

CPSIA compliance information: Batch #CS18W44: For further information contact
Enslow Publishing LLC, New York, New York at 1-800-542-2595.

For mi prima, always.

O s m e l

IN THE ORCHARD

In the orchard picking
his last bag of apples
for the day,

tío Jorge lifts his cap
and wipes his face.

Lines form
around his eyes
as he squints.

Tío has been
working in the orchard
for more seasons than
anyone can remember.

The wrinkles
he carries are
like little rays
of the sun.

He tells me how
the years move by
too quickly.

They say
working with my uncle
in the orchard
offers life lessons.

Here:
Mom hopes
I learn what it means
to work hard.

Here:
tío Jorge teaches me
that there is pride
in a job well done.

Here:
I prove to myself
that I am able
to keep my body strong—

and my mind
stronger.

One more year,
I think to myself
as I place another
apple in the bag

that is tied tight
around my
shoulders.

One more year
until I can go
to college.

One year
can't go by

fast enough—

The last box
of apples
is weighed.

Six men
cram into a Toyota
pickup truck
painted the same deep red
as an Empire apple.

We twist
and sway
down the long green
rows

of cherry,

apple, and

pear trees.

The late afternoon air
rushes through the truck bed.

I stretch
out my long legs

after a long day
and close my eyes.

In the breeze,
I pretend to fly

as the air scoops up
the hairs on my
sweaty arms.

There is no breeze
in the rows of trees.

All day my arms
stay covered.

Head covered.
                Mouth covered.

The breeze cannot
find us in the rows
                so covered.

THE MANY SKIES OF WASHINGTON

I rest my head
on the side of the
truck bed.

The bandana I wore
around my face
in the orchard

is now the
cushion between
my head and the
metal truck body.

I feel the
road change
with my body.

The bumpy gravel
of the foothill roads
smooths out

as the truck turns
onto the paved road.

The road that will lead us into
Moses Lake.

The tops of two-
and three-story buildings

peek over the hazy
blue atmosphere.

Down in our valley
town, the sky is
a streaky, dirty window.

In the late summer,
brown soot covers
everyone's eyeballs.

The wildfire
smoke from Quincy,
Wenatchee, and Chelan
rolls east.

And the brown, smoky
soot gets trapped in
the hills.

The skies
of Eastern Washington
are suffering.

I have many
questions

as to how the sky
holds weather.

I have many
questions

about the many
skies of Washington.

I hope in a year
I can be studying

the science of weather
at a college
far away from Moses Lake.

At the University at Washington
west of the Cascade Mountains.

The side of Washington
that the wildfires
never touch.

The green
rainforest side
of the state.

Away from
the high desert
flames
of Moses Lake.

FIESTA

My sister Leslie
is 12 years old today.

In the bathroom
before her party,
I push back my heavy
black curls
and wipe steam
from my thick glasses.

I search
for my face in
the blurry glass.

I scratch my chin
and slap my cheeks
to help the hairs grow in.

I look at myself
again.

The brown eyes
that find me seem
to change every time
I look into them.

Mom is on her tiptoes
cutting onions
when I come downstairs.

I bend down
to give her a kiss
on the cheek.

She likes to remind me
how this time last year,
I was just as tall as her.

"¡*Mijo!*" she says,
breathing heavily
as she works four pans on
the stove.
"Help me get the patio
ready for the party!"

It takes me a second
to figure out

what she is saying
when she speaks so fast
in Spanish.

She gives up
and rolls her
eyes before I
can guess.

She doesn't like
that I'm not as fast
with Spanish as I
used to be.

Mom whips
the kitchen towel
from her shoulder
to point to the

white plastic bag
bursting with pink
and purple decorations.
She says,

"Your job."

"My job?"

"¡*Bueno*!"

I go outside
and plop a purple
tablecloth on
the picnic table.

In the yard between
our two houses,

tío Jorge's two sons
run around squealing
and laughing
like babies do.

The dogs, Guapa and Benny,
bark and chase them
like little dogs do.

Tío Jorge grills
carne asada
for the party.

I know
he will ask me
to help him.

Como hombres.

It's what men do.

But I don't care
too much about learning
to grill.

His sister,
tía Alejandra—Alex—
stands next to him.

She pokes at the meat
and laughs at the babies.

She eyes me from across
the patio.

I can see in her face
from far away
that she is shocked
at how different I look.

This shocked look
is one I am used to now.

A tiny smile spreads
across tía Alex's face.
She waves.

I make my way
over to her
even though I know
that tío will make me
watch over the meat.

"¡Osmel! ¡*Mijo!*" she says
as we bump shoulders
and hug. "¡*Ay, que guapo!*"

Tío Jorge gives me
a hard slap on the back
and pushes me to the front
of the grill.

  I cross my arms
  and wish I had stayed
  over on my side of the yard.

Tía Alex goes on telling
us about the march she was
part of at her law school in
Seattle.

"It was beautiful!
There were hundreds
of Dreamers all together
and all unafraid, *hermano*.
It brought me to tears!"

Tío Jorge sighs
as he picks up his son,
little Angel.

"*Ayyyy,*

hermana,

be careful—

don't cause any problems

for yourself

or the family."

As tío says this,
I can sense
he is holding back
his true anger.

Tía Alex walks away
from him
and grabs a Coke from
the ice cooler.

"Ha! I'm done
keeping secrets!

At school we've now
all come out
as undocumented."

Without fear, she looks
her brother right in the eye
and takes a long sip of soda.

Too busy taking in
their words,
I am not checking
the flames on the grill.

They have grown
as the heat between
my aunt and uncle
grows.

My arm hair
tingles
and the air smells
of burnt me.

This is why
I don't ask to grill.

STING

Tía rushes me
to the round table
and dumps a bucket
of ice over my arm.

Shocking cold
mixes with the
raw, hot patch of skin.

Long drips of water
run down the sides
of the purple plastic
tablecloth.

The dogs yip and
happily lick up the water
and lay in the fresh cool
puddles.

"You'll be okay,"
tía Alex says
over and over.

She is not a mother,
but she could be.

"Want to talk a minute, Osmel?"

she asks as she
pats my arm
with a paper towel.

The seriousness I sense
in her voice is alarming.

But I nod my head
and she shifts
her weight.

"Do you know
what I meant
about being
undocumented?"

"Yeah. It's when you aren't
an American citizen,"

I say. Adding,

"But I didn't know
you were undocumented."

"Why am I not surprised
that they wouldn't tell
you?"

Tía Alex wipes
her face and throws away
her smile.

For the second time
in one minute,
she has me worried.

"Oh, Osmel..." she says
in a low voice.

Her hand smooths
over the wet thumb-sized
burn on my arm.

"You are undocumented, too."

PUNCH

Her words hurt
like a punch in the chest.

I look above her
to the chain-link fence
and the afternoon sky.

A long layer of flat cloud
rolls in front the sun.

If I look at tía's face,
I have to accept
what she is saying
as the truth.

Tía straightens up
in the leaning plastic chair.

"Osmel..."

She says my name low.
She looks at my eyes,
saying nothing more.

Our families.
Our homes.
Our lives.

I know
that my family
came to the United States
by crossing the border
through Texas.

But I thought our whole
family had become
citizens years ago.

We sit at the
round purple
table.

Tía Alex presses
leaking ice
onto my burn.

She gives
my fortune
as she retells my life
like a dream.

She speaks of my
first five years
in Mexico.

She looks me in the
eyes and nods her head
that it is all true.

We came here
by crossing with Coyotes,
smugglers.

I am not a true citizen
of the United States.

Deep down
I remember Mexico,
but I choose not to
think about that place.

I don't
understand why
no one ever told me
the truth.

Why today?
This random day—
as people arrive
for the party.

I can hear them
gathering.

"What about Leslie?"
I ask.
Tía looks up
to the heavy sky
like she
might have felt
a drop of rain.

"Leslie was born
in Washington.

She is a citizen, Osmel.
Your sister
is an American."

PIÑATA

¡*Dale, dale, dale!*   Hit it, hit it, hit it!

No pierdas tu objetivo,   Don't lose your aim,

porque si lo pierdes,   because if you lose it,

pierdes el camino.   you will lose the way.

¿*Dónde?* ¿*Dónde?*

I think.

                                Where? Where?

📍

I take off the blindfold. Sight turns

from darkness to a swirl of yellow candies

scattering like popcorn across

the

patio.

Cousins and candy everywhere!

Finally!

I dive in

scraping my knees on the concrete.

Marta steps on my hands.

"¡*Ay*! Watch yourself!"

Maria and Valentina
        scoop up *dulces* in their arms
        and fall to the ground laughing.

Luis and Angel
        claw like hawks for candy.

I scurry for the *rebanaditas*, my favorite.

Tío Jorge and tía Alex
        dump the piñata and throw more candy.

¡AYYYYYY!

A wave of children squeal as sweets
shower from above.

I open my mouth to catch a piece.

But it bounces off my tooth

and makes its way from the air

into the hand of little Angel.

O s m e l

BETWEEN LANDS

How ironic that Leslie is
a citizen, and I am not.

My favorite holiday
has always been
the Fourth of July.

The time of year
when the cherries are sweet
and we spend our days
floating down the river.

On the Fourth, we eat
red, white, and blue Popsicles.

We lay with the dogs
on the concrete
to keep our skin cool.

Red, white, and blue
sugar water drips
down our hands
for the dogs
to catch.

When I was younger,
I would save
the Popsicle sticks
with jokes written
on the ends.

I would tell them
to my family.

But they never laughed
at these jokes in English.

They still don't laugh
at my jokes.

These days, I don't laugh
at their jokes in Spanish,
either.

HER LAND

Leslie speaks Spanish
with Mom.

She calls her *mamá*
and calls her dog *Guapa*.

She sings to Los Tigres del Norte
with tía Carmen and tío Jorge

as if she grew up
in Michoacán.

Instead of me.

Leslie goes
to Spanish culture club
after school

and dances
twice a week with
the Baile Foklórico
dancers.

Leslie asks
to learn the recipes
and the prayers.

She cries for our dad
and speaks about him
like she knew him.

She has always
been this way,

which suddenly
makes it hard for me
to be around her.

DISTANCE

Mom asked me
to pick up Leslie
from Spanish culture club
every Tuesday.

I wait for her
in the front hallway
of the school

and watch
storm chaser videos
on my phone.

When Leslie comes down
the rows of lockers,

she and her friends
dance and laugh
so loud

that their voices
bounce off the white-
tiled walls.

The only girl in the group
I've seen before
is Valentina Hernandez,
Rodrigo's cousin.

They all look
like babies to me.

With her round
Muñoz face and
pink ribbons wrapped
above her ponytail,

Leslie looks
the youngest
of them all.

So innocent.

So free.

It is a mile-and-a-half
walk home under the hot,
streaky, smoke-filled sky.

I don't
want to ask
Leslie about her day.

And yet
I find the question leaking
out of my mouth.

"I think I really like
my teachers this year,"
she says, looking up at me.

"And most of my
best friends
are in my homeroom.
Mr. Lawrence doesn't
even care if we talk too loud."

Beyond this
simple question,
I don't have anything
to say to her right now.

♀

Two little
dogs follow us
down Canal Street.

Dogs without
collars or tags
can move along quietly.

Sometimes Leslie
calls to these dogs—

dogs that don't
belong to anyone.

Sometimes she wants
to take them home.

Sometimes she
names them:
Chula, Guapa, Princesa.

Sometimes I
go along with her
and think about bringing
them home.

44

Dogs like this
come and go
in Moses Lake.

They dip between houses
and find other scrappy
friends to follow for
awhile.

We make
our way down
Methow, Peachy,
and Ferry streets.
We cut through
the dirt paths,

past old
pickup trucks and

dust-covered
concrete yards.

It is 4:30
and the sun is still smack
in the middle of
the sky.

I want to
walk faster. But my
feet are too sweaty
to pick up
and put down
without my sock
sliding out from
my shoes.

In the desert valley,
apple country.

It's crazy to think
these are two in the same
place.

Like me and Leslie.

HURRICANE HEAD

Yesterday Mariana
told Rodrigo
she didn't want
to date him anymore.

During lunch today, he says
that nothing looks
the same to him now.

He says that his heart
is like a trapdoor—

he never knows when
the door might open
and he will fall through it.

A stomach-dropping
sadness.

I want to tell him
that I feel worse
than he does.

I look around the lunch table.
How do I ask my friends
where they were born?

Rodrigo and
Juan and
Jose and
Eric and
Jessica and
Maribel?

Can they tell
that I don't have papers?

Can they tell
that I am
undocumented?

Julia waits for me
at the bottom of the
stairs after lunch.

We've always been friends,
but this year we have
a few of the same classes.

She's easy to talk to.

Getting to see her in class
is the only reason I've
been coming to school
lately.

When I see her,
she asks what's up.

I say, "Nothing,"
and make a joke.

This is something
I'm too good at doing.

TÍA ALEX TEXTS

8:49 p.m.   Hey Osmel! I'm coming home tomorrow
            for Dias. You wanna grab *lunche*?

8:50 p.m.   Yeah! When?

Tía Alex pulls up
to school
in her silver truck.

She turns down
the Juan Gabriel song
"*Abrazame Muy Fuerte*"
and smiles real big.

"*¡Hola sobrino!*"
she says, happily.

I put my backpack
in the back seat
and climb in.

♦

"Boy, you need to eat!
You look so thin
since last month.

What did you do?
Get a girlfriend, *chico*?"
she asks,
          smacking her gum.

"Naaah, tía."
I wish.

Through the blue mirror
of her sunglasses,
I can sense her eyes
meeting mine.

She whips
her head forward
and cranks the truck
into second gear.

"Yeah, I saw
your text wanting
to know more about
DACA, the college program,"
she says.

I sigh,
"Yeah, that was two
weeks ago."

Two weeks of worry.

She looks
back over to me.

"*Mi culpa*,
Osmel, I'm sorry."

"It's all good," I lie to her,
as I make room for my knees
under the crammed dashboard—

suddenly wishing I was
anywhere else but here.

HOT NOODLES

With hot noodles
in front of us
and two bottles of Coke,

we are ready
to really talk.

Tía begins by scratching
her face,

as if struggling in
a debate with another
law student at school.

She looks too old
to be 25. She has worried
too much in her life.

"Remember how I said
no one knows
what's going on
in our family
when it comes

to our status in the U.S.?"
she asks,
with her hand resting
on her chin.

"Yeah," I say,
as I eat my noodles.

"I want to change that.

I want to help
everyone know
their rights.

Get you set up
for an education.
I know my *hermana*
thinks college
just comes with good grades.

But she didn't see
what a struggle
it was for me
to get where I am."

Tía tells me
more about DACA:
Deferred Action for Childhood Arrivals.

Tía was able to get into
law school because of DACA.

She says that because
we came to the U.S.
when we were very young,
this legal paper allows us
to study in college and remain safe.

"So the government can't
send me back to Mexico, then?"

Tía smiles and nods while
eating the last of her noodles.

"You've got it!"

Tía gives me
the name of a
social worker who
can help me
apply for DACA.

Guadalupe Soledad.

GUADALUPE

has an office
that was once a
closet.

Over her desk
there are two flags:

a Mexican
flag

and a small red one
with a
big black bird on it.

"You know
of Cesar Chavez?"

asks the woman
with big wild
curls and a belly
round with a baby.

I smile. "Yeah—sort of.

That's his flag
right? For the Farm
Workers' Union?"

She nods and gives
me a wink.

"Do you have family
who work in the orchards
or packing sheds?"

The very pregnant
Guadalupe, who
said to call her Lupe,
sits down on a folding chair.

She points
to another in the corner
for me.

"I work at Garrett
Orchards sometimes
with my uncle.

My mom and aunts
work in the packing
sheds," I say.

Lupe nods and winks
again, writing something
about my life
on a pink Post-It note.

"And did you know
I had an office in
the school?" she asks.

"No," I say.

Lupe pretends to
slam her head
on her desk.

"How did I miss you?"
she yells,
with her curly hair
waving madly.

We laugh
uncomfortably.

She throws
up her hands
and looks to me.

"How can I help you?"

I ask her
about DACA.

Lupe's eyes lower.
She puts her pen
down.

"You are undocumented, yes?"

I nod my head.
Lupe takes a breath.
"Osmel, DACA would
have been an option for you...
but the program is no
longer accepting new—"

I crack my neck
side to side and sigh.

I can tell from
her sad face that my
sigh was loud enough
for her to hear.

"It would have allowed
you to live in the U.S.
and go to college.

But even so, DACA was
not a way to becoming
a U.S. citizen."

Lupe reaches over
and pats my shoulder.

Her eyes
are like my mother's.

"*Mijo*, you
can still go to college
in Washington.

Most schools here
don't ask how
you got here—

I can help
you find a school
if that's what
you want,"
she says.

"I would like that,"
I say. I wanted to go to
University at Washington
in Seattle anyway.

She smiles.

"What would you like
to study, Osmel?" she asks.

"The weather," I say.

WEATHERMAN

My favorite year
of school was
the fifth grade.

The first day
of that year,

I read a book
about storm chasing.

And then I read
a book about tornadoes.

And then one on
hurricanes.

I still feel
the same excitement
when thinking about
crazy weather now

as I did
when I first read
those books.

I would look
at the pictures
for hours.

By the time Mr. Rawhaus
taught us about clouds
and the atmosphere,
I already knew it all.

Mr. Rawhaus
was impressed.

He and I would
talk about hurricanes

and tornadoes
and how they form.

I made a mini tornado
in a soda bottle

for my science project
that year.

Mr. Rawhaus called
me the class
meteorologist.

It took me two weeks
to remember how to say
that word: meteorologist.

A weatherman.

That was years ago,
but that's still
what I want to be.

It's still my dream.

SUNNY-SIDE UP

On Saturday morning,
Mom cooks eggs.

She makes them
sunny-side up
with one square

of orange cheese
placed over
the yolk.

"Osmel, you're not
eating your eggs.

You're upset,"
she yells in Spanish.

Mom puts
orange juice
on the table
and moves closer.

With her hair
pulled back tight,
she bends down
and stares at me.

Tiny wrinkles pop
out of her forehead
over her thin, painted
eyebrows.

"I'm not mad
or anything," I say

as I scratch
my plate with
my fork.

I am just starting
to feel like
I am able to
swallow my
undocumented life.

But I don't
want to talk to her
about it.

After all, she lied
to me for this long.

Mom takes a
sip of juice
and digs deeper
into my mood.

"*Mijo*, Leslie says
you're not talking
to her.

Why? You love
your sister.

She needs
her big brother.
      You know that—"

I look down
at the egg I have
left.

The yellow yolk
slowly leaks out.

A red pressure
builds in my head
as she stares at me.

I could scream.
I imagine spilling
her orange juice
everywhere.

How I would just
walk away,

juice leaking over
the sides of the purple
tablecloth.

But I do not spill
her juice or let
my anger take over
like a flame.

Instead, I stay
quiet and spoon
up my yolk.

Mom stays sitting
and turns her chair

away from me.
From this angle,
she looks like a
powerful hawk.

Her big searching
eyes and smooth
black hair shine.

In this moment,
I remember
that Mom has
a name of her own.

She has a life
and a story
that I'll never
know.

I think about
her journey
here
and how little

I understand.
She must
have brought me
to Washington
alone.

With Leslie big
in her belly.
How did she
hold onto me
all that time?

How did she
get me across
the river?

I get up
from the table

and kiss her on the
crown of her head.
I wash my dish
and keep quiet.

📍

Mom's phone rings—
It's tía Carmen.

They make plans
for lunch.

Benny and Guapa's tiny paws
skitter across the kitchen
floor as the door opens.

Tío Jorge walks in
with Angel and Luis.

One in each arm.
Giggling bubbles
of baby joy.

Leslie and Valentina
rush downstairs
to greet them.

Suddenly life moves
past another angry moment.

DÍA DE LOS MUERTOS

Leslie wears a long dress
when she dances
at the community center.

Mom used to dance
the same dances in
Mexico, she tells us.

Now she braids
her daughter's
hair in the same way
she once wore.

Tonight, Mom draws
a black and white skull
on half of Leslie's face
and puts big golden
flowers behind her ears.

It is the time of year again
when the dark comes earlier
and the wind picks up.

Día de los Muertos.
Day of the Dead.

Mom, tía Carmen,
and tía Alex

sit around
our kitchen table
preparing decorations.

With tiny scissors,
they make small
paper flags of many colors.

Little bits of rainbow
paper fall from their busy
hands to the floor.

The paper is then quickly
swept up into bags.

I want to help
by throwing the bags
in the trash.

Mom sticks out her hand
to stop me.

"The scraps can be used
as confetti to place
around altars," she says.

They will make the altars
from tables and boxes
covered in cloth.

It's tradition.

At the community center,
I help set up chairs
and tables.

I pour Coke
and *horchata*
into tiny paper cups.

I watch Leslie
as she unfolds a blue
blanket and places it
over the small table
set for our family altar.

Mom and my aunts hang
the rainbow paper flags
around the room,
strand by strand.

They place sweet bread
on napkins around
tall candles and the pictures
of my father and grandparents.

HOPE FOR THE DREAM

I am thinking
a lot about all
the things Lupe
said.

I stop by
Lupe's closet office
most days after math.

She gives me
dulces.

She tells me
more about being
an undocumented person.

A Dreamer.

Lupe says there are many
young people like me
who live here
undocumented.

At least
I am not alone.

Dreamer.
Dreamer.
Dreamer.

I say it

in my head

to get used
to the sound.

Like maybe
it will make things
easier.

Butterflies
are the symbol for
the movement.

Tonight, for the celebration,
my sister is dressed
like one.

Leslie stands with
her friends,
wearing bright colors.

How many of the
people I know here
are Dreamers
like me?

Sometimes I want to
scream out
and share the confusion
that I live in.

Before I walk home,
I visit the altar that's wrapped
in a blue blanket.

I am met by a face
like my own
in a gold frame

In the picture, Juan
Osmel Lopez Aveja
stands next to a truck
on an orange dusty road.

He wears
a black baseball cap.

I stare into the eyes
of this man

and try to remember
how to love him.

My father is a symbol
of a life I don't
remember.

His bones rest
in Michoacán, but
we remember
him thousands
of miles away.

I feel Leslie's
eyes on me from
the stage.

She's up there.
And I'm down here.

So I say a quick prayer
at the altar.

Keep us safe here, Dad.

L e s l i e

PAST AND PRESENT

I dance

for Michoacán,
the state in Mexico
where my family lived
for as long as mamá
can remember.

I dance

for the Muñoz family
of my mother,
and Lopez family
of my father.

Two families
of farming people.

I like to think
we are very strong people.

When my mamá
does my braids up
and puts an orange
flower in my hair,

she gives me a part
of herself to carry
onto the stage.

My feet stomp.
My heart is full of pride.

I smile bright when we move
around the wooden stage.

I sway my shoulders
back and forth.

I hold onto the skirts
that sweep to my ankles,
wide as a blanket.

When I spin my body,
I am a hurricane.

I twirl with my hands out.
I meet my partner in the center.
I stomp with my right foot

before I come back
to twirl once more.
Then I bring my hands
close to me.

I dance for Mexico.
I dance for my family.
I dance for my father.
I dance with bright
colors of hope.

When the music stops,
I am strong as I raise my arms
to the sky
and stop.

I dance
and I am reminded
that I come from
people of love.

O s m e l

HALLOWEEN

On Saturday night,
I meet up with
Rodrigo and Juan.

We all gather
at the gas station
on the corner of
7th Street.

Rodrigo tells us
about a Halloween party
his friend from
the soccer team
is having.

Excitement shoots
through my arms
and head.

I have always loved
Halloween.

I dressed up
as Superman
every year until
the sixth grade.

"Wanna go?"
Rodrigo asks with a sly smile
as he opens his bag
of Takis with a loud pop.

Juan and I
give a little side smile
and agree that we
want to go to a party.

Rodrigo's face beams
like a shiny balloon
in the sun
as he punches
my shoulder hard.

"Wooo!
We're gonna PARTY!"
he yells.

His voice is so loud
that the gas station clerk
comes out from behind her counter.
She stares at us with arms crossed.
We laugh even louder.

We put up our hoods
and walk into the crisp
fall air.

📍

At Rodrigo's house,
we decide to look
for costumes to wear.

Juan picks out
his soccer jersey
from middle school
with black and orange lettering.

Rodrigo tries on
a green T-shirt
and his sister's
curly green wig.

I keep on my
white Nikes
and white T-shirt.

I look around the
bathroom and put
a white bath towel
over my head.

I'm a ghost!

Juan and Rodrigo
hold their sides
from laughing
when I come out
of the bathroom.

I duck under
the doorframe
with the towel
on my head.

And I laugh right back
at them.

Rodrigo's big green
wig bounces
around on his wide shoulders
and stocky body.

I can't breathe because
my stomach hurts
too much from laughing.

I try to tell Rodrigo
that he looks like a big piece
of broccoli.

"Oh yeah?"
he says back.

"Well, you look like
Lebron James's ghost
with those kicks!"

"Yeah!" says Juan.

"More like Lebron's
skeleton ghost.
You are so *flaco*!"

We laugh and
share a can of
Rodrigo's dad's
beer that he snuck
out of the garage fridge.

📍

Our older friend
Carlos picks us up
to go to
the party.

We squeeze
into the back seat.

The broccoli,

the ghost,

and the soccer player.

Buzzed off a sip
of beer.

As we drive away,
I become nervous.

Will we be
the only Mexican guys
at the party?

Will the four of us
get pulled over
because of the color
of our skin?

Then I become
not nervous but
flat-out scared.

Scared that my friends
are like me.

Are they Dreamers, too?

Should we even be here
celebrating Halloween?
Or should we be hiding
like ghosts?

LATE NOVEMBER SHED

The orchard is in a state
of clearing.

On Saturday, we clear
the fields of dead branches.

Tío Jorge and Mr. Pancho
are the last two working
in the fields for
the season.

Out in the cold,
they gather
the fallen.

We cannot burn
these branches
because they have
been sprayed with
chemicals.

The chemicals
make sure bugs
do not harm the fruit
while it grows.

But the white,
toxic powder
sticks to the branches
like sap.

It sticks around
long after the last
apple rots away.

We place the piles
of branches at the beginnings
of the endless rows.

I still do not know
just how far
the rows of trees go.

I help tío Jorge and Mr. Pancho
feed branches
through the wood chipper.

We will put
the sawdust
we make
around the base
of the trees.

This will help keep
them warm
in winter.

The three of us
work under the dreamy,
high clouds
of late November.

📍

"There is a tropical storm
gathering in the gulf.
It will hit Puerto Rico
and Cuba soon,"

I tell tío Jorge.
But he has become
distracted.

He looks down the rows
of bare trees.

I watch the pencil point
of brown color
in his eyeball flicker.

Pancho appears
from three rows over.

He knows that when
his friend stops talking,
there is something wrong.

I want to keep gathering
branches, get the work done.

But a silence
has fallen over us all.

I feel as if
I should turn
into a cold drop of rain

and sink into
the cold, hard earth.

"*Mira*," whispers tío Jorge.

Pancho looks like a deer
in his black wool
hat and a thick tan jacket.

He looks to us
and then out far
over the orchard
with focused eyes.

I try to find
where they are looking.

I cannot see anything
through the rows of earth
and sky cut with thousands
of lines.

My heart beats thick
in my ears
as I look forward.

I hear an engine
turn over.

The noise comes from
beyond the ditch
that runs along
the back of the orchard.

Then
I spot it.

A black SUV
starts to drive away
from us.

It the size of my thumb from
where we stand.

The car must have
been parked,

and it is not even
driving on a road.

THE MOUNTAIN LION

In fifth grade,
we had to choose
an animal to study
and write about.

I still remember
every detail of the book
I chose—

Mountain Lions.

When I read
Mountain Lions,
tío Jorge told me
to never go up
into the foothills alone.

When I asked him why,
he said that people
are killed
by this big cat
in the summer
sometimes.

Mountain lions
look like house cats,
but 10 times bigger.

The animals
they hunt can be
10 times bigger, too.

They watch
the animals they want
to eat for hours, days,
even weeks.

They wait hushed
in trees or behind
big rocks.

Then they pounce
when the animal doesn't
see them coming.

I could sense
the power and danger
of that SUV
like it was a mountain lion.

BACK UP

During homeroom, Julia
asks me about my weekend.

I tell her about
the ICE scare at the orchard.

She tells me to back up.
"What's ICE?"

"Like in your cup,"
I say jokingly.

She folds her arms
and purses her lips.

"No, really,"
she says.

"I feel like such a loner
when you and Juan and Rodrigo
talk about these ICE people."

"You know, they're the
government dudes
who want to kick Mexican kids
like me out of the country,"

I say, failing hard
as I try to make a joke
of my life.

Julia cuts straight to
the part of my joke
that is true.

"Why would these
government agents kick
you out?"

I tell her what I know.

They work for the government
and they find people who look
like me and speak Spanish.

They deport people—
take them from their
families and make them
leave the U.S.

They send us back "home"

even if it's dangerous,
and we hardly remember
living there.
All because we came here
without asking
the U.S. government.

Julia's face drops.

I can't stop my heart
from telling her everything.

I tell her that life
in Michoacán got hard.

When she asks why,
I tell her how they couldn't
get medicine for
my dad in our small town.

He died when I was five.
And we traveled to Washington
that same year.

Julia never stops listening.

She moves her chair closer
to me and wraps her arm around
my shoulder.

"I won't let ICE take you anywhere,"
she says.

WORRY

"Did you see the SUV again,
Jorge?"
asks tía Carmen at dinner.

Every night at dinner,
she asks the questions
that no one else dares
to say out loud.

Mom
keeps her hands on her lap
so we cannot see
if they are shaky.

Tío cuts a chicken *tamal*
into tiny pieces
for Angel and Luis.

"Not today—*gracias a Dios.*"

ICE officers
have come around before.

I have heard stories
of these police-like
men and women.

One time last fall,
ICE came to the packing
shed one town over.

Ten mothers
were taken
to holding centers.

WE THE PEOPLE

We have been learning
about the Constitution
in U.S. History.

This old paper
makes me feel insane

as I tear the corners
of my textbook
under my desk.

I look around
the classroom.

A mix of light skin
and dark skin like mine.

Mrs. Erikson
is white.

She tries hard
to make sure we
do well in her class.

She tells the class
that she chooses
not to see the color
of people's skin.

You can't teach
U.S. history if
you choose not
to see racial differences.

The fourth amendment
reads that we have the right
to private property.

Do I?

The fifth amendment
reads that we have the right
to keep silent when approached
by police.

It also says we
have the right to go
to court instead of being
thrown right in jail.

Do I have these rights?

I am trying hard
not to get upset
as Mrs. Erikson
keeps saying "we"
in class.

As if "we"
all have the same rights.

I need to know
if the Constitution,
the amendments,

apply to them
more than me.

Lupe would know.
I want to ask
her so many things—

but she hasn't
been in her office
all week.

Tía Carmen
and Mom are speaking
in Spanish.

I cannot hear
what they are saying
other than "ICE."

I fear that ICE agents
are getting closer
to our community
in Moses Lake.

What do they have against
orchard workers
and fruit packers
and weather geeks?

EVERY DAY

when I wake up,
the world is blurry.

I take the black,
square glasses
from my nightstand
and reach for my phone.

I text Juan to wake up
and push out of my twin bed.

I look out the window
to the grey, high sky.

Guapa and Benny
bark.

I hear the babies
crying.

I hear my aunt
singing.

And my sister
in the shower.

I use the bathroom
by the kitchen
and brush my teeth
and wash my face.

I look up
in the mirror
at the tiny scars
and the red marks
around my nose.

Imagine what I would
look like in a holding center.

I take oil
and I slick
back my curls.

In the kitchen,
I read a note
from Mom:

"Make today a good one."

I text Juan again to wake up.
It's his last warning.

I check the weather.
Breezy and cold.

I put on
my heavy jacket

and put up
the hood.

I grab my
backpack

sitting by the
back door.

I shut the door.
Lock it up.

📍

I remember
something

and unlock
the door.

I run
to the bottom
of the stairs

and yell up
to my family.

I tell them
that I love them,

just in case
I can't come home.

I do this
every day

now that ICE is close by.

"OSMEL, CAN WE TALK?"

Our feet stomp
to a stop on the wooden
gym floor.

Juan asks again,
"Osmel, can we talk?"

I can't tell
from Juan's breathing
if he is worried

or just wants to talk
about baseball.

"Of course, man," I say,
slapping him on the back.

"After school," he says.

Juan keeps his eyes
on the floor
as we walk out into
the crowded hallway.

The bell rings
for the end of the day.

The hallway fills
up quickly and we
have to push our way to
the front doors.

The cold December air
slaps our faces.

The sidewalks are
slippery,

so we walk
in the street.

I want to be
Juan's shadow.

As I walk
a few steps
behind him,

I want to be
whatever he needs.

We make our way
to the gas station
and buy Takis and soda.

We sit on
the frozen bench
outside.

Juan is still quiet.

I take my phone
out of my jacket pocket
and check the weather.

It's 28 degrees.

📍

"*Mi padre*
didn't come home
last night."

Juan shifts
his weight.

His legs swing
a little off the ground.

We let these words
set in.

Now I know why
it was so hard for Juan
to speak.

We eat our chips
mindlessly.

We drink our sodas
in 30 seconds.

"He was driving
to get a tractor
up in Quincy.
Got pulled over."

Juan takes another sip
before twisting the cap
back on tight enough
to break the bottle.

"He called my mom
from a holding center.
I don't know if he'll be back."

I smile. I don't know why,
but I smile.

Like it's all
gonna work out.

I raise a handful
of chips to my mouth.
But I am not hungry.

I feel horrible.

RED AND BLUE LIGHTS IN
THE REARVIEW MIRROR

Turn around,
see the swirling—

sound of the sirens
takes all the breath
out of you.

Don't say anything.

        Don't say anything.

Take the red
card out from
your wallet.

And if they try
to take you
away,

say something.   Tell them:

"I have rights, sir."

Juan's reality
breaks everything open.

Juan's dad is a serious man.
Built like a stone.
Strong and unshakable.

I imagine his steady face
as he was approached by ICE officers.

This scene replays
in my mind all night.

Sometimes I picture
tío's face
in place of Juan's dad—
and even my own.

It's a nightmare, but I am
still awake.

In the morning, I walk
the six blocks to Juan's
apartment building.

Usually I find Juan
waiting outside.

Today he's not.

When I'm buzzed in,
I find him still in bed.

Rodrigo is standing
at the dresser,
throwing clothes
at our friend.

"Get dressed!"

Juan is slow
to get ready.
So we talk.

There's no joke to
be made.

On this random
freezing Tuesday morning,
we finally *talk*.

Rodrigo asks Juan
the heavy question.

Is he undocumented?

Juan nods his head yes.

"I was trying
to get my working papers
and found out."

I must look weird,
because they look at
me.

"You too?" Juan asks.

I bob my head. Say, "Yeah."

There is silence.

"I asked *mi papá* a few
years ago. Straight out
was brutal and asked him
if our family had citizenship,"

Rodrigo says quietly.

"He told me we
have a visa for his job.
It's not citizenship—but it's
something—"

We agree.
It is something.

"I'm going to help you
figure this out," Rodrigo says
to me and Juan.

"I'm here," he says, taking
us in a double headlock.

On this random
freezing Tuesday morning,
we finally *talk*.

SOUNDS OF COMFORT

Chicken *tamales*
and cinnamon tea
heal my stomach
when it turns sour
from thinking
too much.

I hear tío Jorge's truck
pull up on the gravel
and turn off.

There is peace in this,
these simple sounds:

tío coming home.
       His bootsteps.

The sound of his keys
as they lift to open
his front door.

Juan's dad
is being held in
Olympia, Washington.

Mamá says
we will bring
tamales to their apartment.

It is the second night
of Posadas.

We travel from house
to house

remembering the story
of Christmas.

I know that to be
in a holding center
is much like being put in jail.

waiting
                    waiting
                                        waiting

For three weeks
he has been waiting.

His family
is waiting, too.

When we arrive with the food,
we don't ring their doorbell.

We know to call
Juan's mamá on her phone.

These days, a knock
at the door could be ICE.

"We have to do what we can
to help each other,"
mamá says.

I wonder if
Juan's mamá would come
to my door
with *tamales*
one day to comfort me if…

O s m e l

FEVER

I sleep
on and off
and text Julia.

She says she hopes
I feel better soon.

Coughing heavy,
I drift away, wondering
if she likes me more than
as a friend.

Just when I
fall into a dream,

Mom opens my door
to check on me.

She places her hands
on my head and
says that the VIX rub
and soup have cured me.

I moan and say
that she is lying.

I feel just as sick
as I did in gym
on Tuesday, when I
threw up in the locker room
in front of all the guys.

Slowly I turn over
and tell my mom
to go away.

PAIN

It is an icy night
and the moon is
hanging above Moses Lake
like a silver cut.

There are only two
clouds in the west
to keep her company.

It is too cold
for the stars to dance with her.

But the moon,
the brave moon,
she is constant
and courageous.

Leslie said she
got out of the Chevy
and rushed ahead

as mom walked behind
her. Tried to get out
of the cold quickly,
                    quickly.

Leslie grabbed
a shopping cart
and made her way
to the front doors
of the store.
On her way
to get me medicine.

Then Leslie said

she was looking down

          she was looking down at Mom

                    she was looking down at Mom on the icy
                    black ground.

📍

Leslie cries
as she tells me
the details of
Mom's fall.

She called me
as soon as it
happened, and
I got there.

The little moon
looks down

on us: brother and sister
in the blue night.

The cloud of
fumes from
the running ambulance
chokes us
as we wait.

My stomach
grows more sour
with every breath.

"I'm really sorry,"
Leslie says, burying her
neck into her pink jacket.

"Why?" I ask.

"Because I think I did this."

Leslie looks at me
and cries as
she holds up her
phone.

"I called them here."

THE BREAKDOWN

I turn my back
to her.

My body
tenses up

from my neck
down to my wrists.

My anger can
come on so quickly.

"You know the
police come when
you call 911,"
I spit.

I can hear Leslie
starting to sob.

"I didn't think about it,"
she says.

"They'll ask for
Mom's papers. And she
doesn't have any, Leslie,"

I add, cutting off her
cries.

I don't have anything
in my wallet that proves
I belong here either.

More than ever before,
I am scared.

We might never go
home again.

I want to
fall onto the ground
and scream.

But silence,
and acting as if I belong,
are my best defenses.

Leslie doesn't
have to pretend
that she belongs.

She can go on
crying like a baby.

She'll grab the attention
of some white EMT
worker.

Then they can question
us even more.

All the envy I've held
for her freedom for months
comes out in one bite.

"You're more
of an idiot than I
thought,"

I say to Leslie,
and I walk away.

I go sit on the
curb and wait
for our fate.

BIENVENIDA: WELCOME

Turning onto our street
in tío's truck, I see
everything through new eyes.

I notice
the sound

of loose rocks
under my feet.

I walk through
the front gate

that leads
to our house.

Guapa and Benny
bark at the door.

I stop and
take in the night.

The warm glow
of the open door

and the old painted sign
that reads,

"*Bienvenida*:
        Welcome."

For tonight,
we are safe.

Mom is
not badly hurt.

I hold on
to the truth
in these words.

Tío Jorge
takes me by the
shoulders.

He shakes me
as we enter the house.

"We will be okay,"
he says.

Mom tells
us
that she
was scared.

She was grateful
the responders didn't ask
for her health insurance.

They only asked
for her address
and her name.

"So the responders
know where we live?"

I ask, imagining ICE
agents circling
our house as we sleep.

I can't look
at Leslie.

She buries her face
into Mom's shoulder.

Tía Carmen
helps Mom upstairs
to bed.

I kiss Mom's head
and smooth her hair.

She looks me
in the eye. Says,

"We will be okay, *mijo*."

Later on,
when the house
grows dark,

I will bring a blanket
and sleep downstairs.

Just in case.

HAY OPCIONES—
THERE ARE OPTIONS

When tía Alex heard
about Mom's fall at Safeway,
she came straight home
from Seattle.

She arrives at
our door

with a bag of chips
and a cake.

"Muriel, *necesitamos hablar,*"
she says.

We need to talk.

Mom is resting
on the couch
when tía arrives.

She stands up slowly
to kiss her sister hello.

Mom shakes her blanket,
smooths her pale
purple blouse,
and sits back down.

Tía does the same.

I have been sitting
on the couch next to Mom.
Texting Julia, Rodrigo, and Juan.

I stand up to give tía a hug
and try to leave the room
for the talk in Spanish that
will soon take place.

"*Mijo*,"

tía says with a smooth,
even voice.
"Sit with us for awhile."

Leslie stands
in the corner,

as still
as a houseplant.

She holds Guapa
in her arms
like a doll.

Tía Alex goes
into the kitchen
and brings us slices
of cake.

We wait for her
and we do not speak.

As tía Alex hands
us plates of cake,
she begins.

"Muriel, I am scared for you
and Jorge and Carmen
and Osmel."

Mom's eyes shoot
over to me and fill
to the top with pain.

I look at her
and then quickly
look down
at my cake.

Tía Alex says,

"He knows
he knows
he knows

that he's undocumented."

And this is when,
for the first time
in a long time,
I watch Mom cry.

"What have I done?"

Mom says slowly
in Spanish.

She says it again.

Once to her sister,
and then to me,
and then to Leslie.

I look away.

Leslie looks away.

Tía Alex pushes
her small body forward.

She looks
like a father

with her elbows square
on her lap

and her shoulders
stretched out.

"I have been thinking
 the same thing, *hermana*.

What have I done?

I've hid away at school
for too long.
I've read, studied, and lived
immigration law.

I've built myself up
with other Dreamers
on campus
while neglecting
my family of Dreamers here."

Tía Alex takes a breath
and speaks again.

"There are
so many things
we can call mistakes,

but are they worth
punishing yourself
over every day?

Are they, Muriel?"

Tía Alex holds her breath
and waits.

"I don't know,

     I don't know,"

     Mom whispers
     to the room.

With this honest
exchange, tía
falls into the arms
of her sister.

Leslie runs to them
and smooths
tía's short hair.

She rubs her back
with small pats

up and down
her spine.

I sit still
and helpless
like a box
no one can open.

TWO WORLDS

I live in a twofold
world.

By day, it's all good.

I've got my mind
on weather systems,
Julia, and the next test
I have to take.

At night,
this other world
appears.

Fear creeps in
when I turn out
the light over my bed.

It wraps me into
an endless angry galaxy.

One thousand swirling
black holes are ready
to suck me in and erase
me from the world I know.

I fear
the future.

I question
all the goals I work
toward during the day.

I question wanting
to date Julia.

Sometimes I think
it is unfair to
like her so much.

*What happens if I'm
deported?*

I question my decision
to study meteorology.

*They don't hire undocumented
meteorologists, do they?*

Fear settles my battle
against the future by
offering easy outs—

*Work at Garret Orchards.
        Make money for the family.
Stay quiet...*

When these thoughts come,

I find strength
in the people who
understand.

I know they live
in this tired twofold
world, too.

Juan, Maribel,
and Lupe...

We are tired.

How much longer
do we have to live in this
back-and-forth between
day and night?

When will
change come?

STEPS

Lupe returns
to Moses Lake High.

She sits
behind her desk
under her two flags.

She shows me
a picture of her baby,
Oscar.

Lupe and I
look at the steps
I need to take to make
it to college.

She prints out
a packet of financial
aid papers.

"Maybe I don't
actually want to go
to college," I say.

Lupe shakes
her head.

"I already told *mi mamá*
she would have
a weatherman
who speaks Spanish
and English.

Don't make me
a liar to *mi mamá*."

She twists
her head to
the side,

sending her curly
hair jumping.

"Tell her I can't
speak Spanish
so great,"

I say, teasing
her as I lean back
on the folding
chair.

Now she gets
my jokes and
laughs in my face.

She says,

"Spanish is in
your blood. It will
come back when
you're ready, Osmel."

OOO-OO-OOOO

I ask Mom
about my social
security number.

She quickly
tells me that she
doesn't know what
I mean.

I ask tío Jorge
about my social
security number.

He says he doesn't
have a real one to
let me use.

Then I ask tía Alex
about my social
security number.

She has an answer.

Tía Alex says
to write

000-00-0000.

I write nine
zeros on the SSN line
of my college application.

Someday I will
have a social
security number.

When I get one,
I will remember it
by heart.

WE STAY HERE

Juan is strong.
He has been working
out every day.
Even after baseball practice.

He is chosen to be
one of the senior captains
for the baseball team.

He's growing
a beard.

One day while
we walk home,

he tells me
that his mom
and sisters

are moving
to Beaverton, Oregon,
to live with *familia*.

He says that Beaverton
protects undocumented
families.

I look at him,
confused.

"Beaverton is called
a sanctuary city,"
he says.

"In sanctuary cities,
the police do not
report to ICE

if they know people
do not have their papers."

At dinner,
I tell my mom
about Juan's family
moving.

I tell her
there are sanctuary cities
all across the country.

"We could move

to one—

if you want—"

I say.

She listens
as she cuts
her *carne*
and feeds it
to the dogs.

She is slow
to collect her words.

"You worry so much.
Try not to live in such fear, *mijo*."

She reaches to me
and takes my hand.
"We are here. We stay here."

SANCTUARY SOMEWHERE

"What does 'sanctuary'
mean to you all?"

Lupe asks
as she opens
a big bag of
Takis

for our after-school
group.

"Is sanctuary like
a shelter?"

asks Jessica. She adds,

"*Mi mamá* talks
about taking sanctuary
with her sisters

at a church
in Arizona.

The church
helped them escape
the fighting

after their
parents were killed
in San Salvador."

Jose says,

"Isn't sanctuary
a tropical paradise?

Baja, California,
is my sanctuary.

I was born there.
I felt at home
in all the palm trees.

No one could
find me
hiding up in
the huge leaves.

I haven't been back
since we left
when I was eight
or nine."

Rodrigo rolls
his shoulders
back with pride, says,

"To me, sanctuary
is the safety
of my family.

Mi papá's work visa
is our sanctuary."

"*Y aqui*,"

Lupe says
with a grin.

"This is your sanctuary, too.
Don't you know
that I wouldn't
let anyone harm you here?"

Some of us
yell out,
"*Sí*, yes."

Some of us
nod and act shy.

Lupe points up
to the eagles. Says,

"We sit under
the eye of mighty
protectors."

An eagle perches
on the Mexican flag.

Another spreads its wings
on the red one
for the United Farm Workers.

An orange and gold
butterfly card is pinned
under the flags.

I say,

"Sanctuary to me
is somewhere…"

I think of
the welcome sign
over our front door
when we came home
that night.

"…with my family."

More words spill
out of me,

but they don't
come out right.

My friends
support me in this.

They know.

♥

Maybe we all feel
the same.

Maybe finding
sanctuary

is finding
other people
who understand.

HOPE BLOOMS

Pears are the first
fruit tree to bring
life

in the new
year.

In the last days
of March,

tío Jorge and I
track the freezing
nights.

We hold
our breath.

We shiver in hope
that the tiny
white flowers

will survive the
last zaps of frost.

It is almost
my birthday.

Like every other year,
I fight to have
pizza for my birthday
dinner.

Tío Jorge usually
raises his voice
at me

because he
loves his grill.

But this year
he backs down.

We have
pizza instead
of *carne asada*.

But he won't let
us go without a
piñata.

I tell him
that I'll be 18.

"I'm too old for
party games, tío,"

I say.

"Never, *sobrino*," he says,
as he slaps my back
and laughs.

He makes me think
we will be celebrating
birthdays in this same
house,
playing the same
party games,

until the end of time.

I choose to believe
this to be true.

L e s l i e

CAKE AND FORGIVENESS

Something snapped
in Osmel the night
I called the ambulance
for mamá.

I have never
seen him this
focused.

He is sure
of what he
wants.

I have also
never known him
to stay angry
at me for so long.

On his birthday,
I finally told
him off.

I'm his *hermana*
for life.

I am
not going
anywhere.

He stood
in the doorway,
cornered.

There was
a sorry look
on his face.

I quickly
handed him
his birthday card.

"*Feliz cumple,
hermano.*"

Later that night,
Osmel brought
me a slice of cake

and ice cream
in a bowl.

He knows I don't like
when the cake
and ice cream
touch.

"*Mi culpa,
hermana*,"

he said in Spanish.

"I've been mean."

"That's for sure,"

I said
with a smile.

O s m e l

POSSIBLE FUTURES

I sit with Lupe
in her office that was
once a closet.

We make lists
of my possible
futures.

There are five
seniors crammed
in her office

without a window
or a fan.

All five of us
have been accepted
to Big Bend
Community College.

Two of us got into
Eastern Washington
University.

Maribel, my friend
who studies harder
than anyone else,

got into Yale
in Connecticut.

They are known
for taking students
who are undocumented.

We meet after school
on Mondays to work
with Lupe.

Four of us are thinking
of going to
community college.

Maribel is sure
about going to Yale.

I did not get
into the University
at Washington in Seattle.

It is the only school
that has the classes

I would need
to become
a meteorologist.

I will wait
and figure out
my plan.

One step
at a time.

I will take
science classes
at community college
and live at home.

I will work
at the orchard

for another two
seasons.

Is this what
I wanted?

No.
But it won't
be bad.

It'll just be
another waiting
game.

Tío Jorge always says
the years move by
quickly.

Lupe says next year
I should reapply
to the University at
Washington.

She'll help
me write a letter
to show them how
bad I want this.

She said she'll
keep helping me
apply until we find
a way to my dream.

GRADUATION DAY

There are
500 of us
wearing gold.

We look like kings
and queens in our
long, royal robes.

We gather outside
on the football field,

waiting to walk
across the stage.

I didn't think
today would feel
special,

but I keep taking
these big breaths
that could turn into
cries.

The principal
gets our attention
up on the stage
they built for today.

Behind him sit
all of our teachers.

He makes a short
speech before
he gives the
microphone
to Maribel.

When she starts to speak,
with her big smile,
I feel a tear roll
down my cheek
onto my gold robe.

She speaks
with a clear voice
and looks at us
with pride.

Out in the sea
of people listening
to her every word,
I wonder if anyone
would guess that
she is undocumented.

"Osmel Lopez Muñoz."

I cross the
stage.

I hold my
diploma.

It is suddenly
all so real.

I have passed
the tests.

I have decided
on Big Bend
Community College.

I have a future
that is better
than okay.

I look up
to the sun
and squint
my eyes.

I know
that if I can
do what I've done
so far,

I can do
anything.

I will become
a meteorologist.

GRADUATION PARTY

Mom puts a gold
tablecloth

on the table outside
and in the kitchen.

Tío Jorge buys
enough *carne*
to feed a pack
of lions.

The twins dance
and run around
the green yard
with the dogs.

Julia is here.

She laughs on
the couch with Leslie.

Juan and Rodrigo and
Maribel come.

Under his baseball
cap and behind
his new beard,

I wonder how
Juan is feeling.

He is living with
his uncle now.

His mom
and sisters moved
last month

to the city
in Oregon that
will keep them safe
from ICE.

Juan mostly talks
to Maribel and Rodrigo.

Lupe comes, too,
with her husband
and baby Oscar.

She hands me
a card with
a butterfly on it.

From one Dreamer
to another.

Love,
Lupe.

I have a lot
of friends

and family
who care

for me more
than the world.

This is my sanctuary.

Estoy con suerte.

I am lucky.

Leslie

LAS CHERRIES

Somehow
we're back to

la temporada de
cherries,

the season
of the cherries.

It is a time
of hard work
on hot days.

It is also
the happiest time.

School is
out.

Our bellies
are full.

We eat fresh
food.

We don't stop
eating.

Kids play
on splash pads

while moms
and dads dip

their feet in the
water and rest

after a long
day in the orchards
and packing sheds.

I walk little Angel
and Luis

over to
the graduation party.

They are
going to give
Osmel his presents.

I made him
a sundial

out of plaster
with gems placed
all around the edges.

I wrapped it
in gold paper
with a red bow.

And on the bottom,
I wrote:

Dream it
and do it.

I think of my brother
and his 18 years so far.

I think of how
he was held by
mi mamá
as they crossed
the river from Mexico
to Texas.

I cannot think
of anyone as brave
as Osmel.

Being undocumented
does not hold
him back.

He is proud to be
a Dreamer.

College man.
Future weatherman.
My brother, Osmel.

WANT TO KEEP READING?

If you liked this book, check out another book
from West 44 Books:

LITTLE PILLS
BY MELODY DODDS

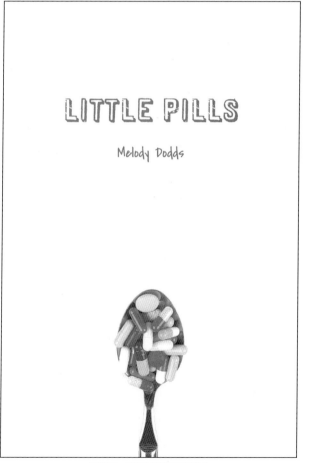

ISBN: 9781538382813

THE SCULPTOR

They say
meth
is   the Monster.

Well.

Oxy   is
an artist who
sculpts
the monster
out of

                                            you.

ESCAPE

The bathroom
is the only place in this house
where I am *guaranteed*
privacy.

So I tend
to spend a

L

O

N

G

time in here.

Let's be clear: I mean "house" in the sense of
home.

House really means
apartment.

Three bedrooms, one bath.
Five people…no, wait.

Four.
Still—
do the math.

Let's be clear: I mean "privacy" in the sense of
walls.

Privacy barely means
solitude.

Someone always needs to use it.

Stay in too long
and they lose it.

But here I am.

No pounding yet
from my mother or
her husband, Rupert.

And no threats
from my sister, Isabella,
who is younger
but whose hunger
to hurt me
is a thing I can't forget.

So I escape.

Check out more books at:
www.west44books.com

An imprint of Enslow Publishing
WEST **44** BOOKS™

ABOUT THE AUTHOR

Brenna Dimmig is a writer and ENL educator. She studied journalism, creative writing, and Spanish at John Carroll University. She lived for several years in the Pacific Northwest as a Jesuit Volunteer. She worked for organizations including Catholic Family and Child Services and El Programa Hispano Católico, where she became familiar with the process of applying for DACA and U.S. Citizenship. She is passionate to share the stories of the families she came to consider her *familia*.